In
1935 if you wanted to
read a good book, you needed
either a lot of money or a library card.
Cheap paperbacks were available, but their
poor production generally mirrored the quality
between the covers. One weekend that year,
Allen Lane, Managing Director of The Bodley Head,
having spent the weekend visiting Agatha Christie,
found himself on a platform at Exeter station trying to
find something to read for his journey back to London.
He was appalled by the quality of the material he had to
choose from. Everything that Allen Lane achieved from that
day until his death in 1970 was based on a passionate belief
in the existence of 'a vast reading public for *intelligent*
books at a low price'. The result of his momentous vision
was the birth not only of Penguin, but of the 'paperback
revolution'. Quality writing became available for the price of
a packet of cigarettes, literature became a mass medium
for the first time, a nation of book-borrowers became a
nation of book-buyers – and the very concept of book
publishing was changed for ever. Those founding
principles – of quality and value, with an overarching
belief in the fundamental importance of reading –
have guided everything the company has
done since 1935. Sir Allen Lane's
pioneering spirit is still very much alive
at Penguin in 2005. Here's to
the next 70 years!

MORE THAN A BUSINESS

'We decided it was time to end the almost customary half-hearted manner in which cheap editions were produced – as though the only people who could possibly want cheap editions must belong to a lower order of intelligence. We, however, believed in the existence in this country of a vast reading public for intelligent books at a low price, and staked everything on it'
Sir Allen Lane, 1902–1970

'The Penguin Books are splendid value for sixpence, so splendid that if other publishers had any sense they would combine against them and suppress them'
George Orwell

'More than a business … a national cultural asset'
Guardian

'When you look at the whole Penguin achievement you know that it constitutes, in action, one of the more democratic successes of our recent social history'
Richard Hoggart

War Talk

PAT BARKER

PENGUIN BOOKS

PENGUIN BOOKS

Published by the Penguin Group
Penguin Books Ltd, 80 Strand, London WC2R ORL, England
Penguin Group (USA) Inc., 375 Hudson Street, New York, New York 10014, USA
Penguin Group (Canada), 10 Alcorn Avenue, Toronto, Ontario, Canada M4V 3B2
(a division of Pearson Penguin Canada Inc.)
Penguin Ireland, 25 St Stephen's Green, Dublin 2, Ireland
(a division of Penguin Books Ltd)
Penguin Group (Australia), 250 Camberwell Road, Camberwell, Victoria 3124,
Australia (a division of Pearson Australia Group Pty Ltd)
Penguin Books India Pvt Ltd, 11 Community Centre,
Panchsheel Park, New Delhi – 110 017, India
Penguin Group (NZ), cnr Airborne and Rosedale Roads, Albany,
Auckland 1310, New Zealand (a division of Pearson New Zealand Ltd)
Penguin Books (South Africa) (Pty) Ltd, 24 Sturdee Avenue,
Rosebank 2196, South Africa

Penguin Books Ltd, Registered Offices: 80 Strand, London WC2R ORL, England

www.penguin.com

Regeneration first published by Viking 1991
Published in Penguin Books 1992
This extract published as a Pocket Penguin 2005

1

Set in 10.5/12.5pt Monotype Dante
Typeset by Palimpsest Book Production Limited
Polmont, Stirlingshire
Printed in England by Clays Ltd, St Ives plc

A short, dark-haired man sidled round the door, blinking in the sudden blaze of sunlight. Sassoon, sitting on the bed, looked up from the golf club he'd been cleaning. 'Yes?'

'I've b-brought these.'

A stammer. Not as bad as some, but bad enough. Sassoon exerted himself to be polite. 'What is it? I can't see.'

Books. *His* book. Five copies, no less. 'My God, a reader.'

'I wondered if you'd b-be k-kind enough to s-sign them?'

'Yes, of course.' Sassoon put the golf club down and reached for his pen. He could have dispatched the job in a few moments, but he sensed that his visitor wanted to talk, and he had after all bought *five* copies. Sassoon was curious. 'Why five? Has the War Office put it on a reading list?'

'They're f-for m-my f-family.'

Oh, dear. Sassoon transferred himself from bed to table and opened the first book. 'What name shall I write?'

'Susan Owen. M-y m-mother.'

Sassoon began to write. Paused. 'Are you . . . quite sure your mother *wants* to be told that "Bert's gone syphilitic?" I had trouble getting them to print that.'

'It w-won't c-come as a sh-shock.'

'Won't it?' One could only speculate on the nature of Mrs Owen's previous acquaintance with Bert.

'I t-tell her everything. In m-my l-letters.'

'Good heavens,' Sassoon said lightly, and turned back to the book.

Owen looked down at the back of Sassoon's neck, where a thin line of khaki was just visible beneath the purple silk of his dressing gown. 'Don't *you*?'

Sassoon opened his mouth and shut it again. 'My brother died at Gallipoli,' he said, at last. 'I think my mother has enough on her plate without any searing revelations from me.'

'I s-suppose she m-must b-be c-concerned about your b-being here.'

'Oh, I don't think so. On the contrary. I believe the thought of my insanity is one of her few consolations.' He glanced up, briefly. 'Better *mad* than a pacifist.' When Owen continued to look blank, he added, 'You do know why I'm here?'

'Yes.'

'And what do you think about that?'

'I agreed with every w-word.'

Sassoon smiled. 'So did my friend Graves.' He opened the next book. 'Who's this one for?'

Owen, feeding the names, would have given anything to say one sentence without stammering. No hope of that – he was far too nervous. Everything about Sassoon intimidated him. His status as a published poet, his height, his good looks, the clipped aristocratic voice, sometimes quick, sometimes halting, but always cold, the bored expression, the way he had of not looking at you when you spoke – shyness, perhaps, but it *seemed* like arrogance. Above all, his reputation for courage. Owen had his own reasons for being sensitive about that.

Sassoon reached the last book. Owen felt the meeting begin to slip away from him. Rather desperately, he said, 'I l-liked "The D-Death B-Bed" b-best.' And suddenly he relaxed. It didn't matter what *this* Sassoon thought about him, since the real Sassoon was in the poems. He quoted, from memory, "'He's young; he hated War, how should he die / When cruel old campaigners win safe through? / But death replied: 'I choose him.' So he went." That's beautiful.'

Sassoon paused in his signing. 'Yes, I – I was quite pleased with that.'

'Oh, and "The Redeemer". "He faced me, reeling in his weariness, / Shouldering his load of planks, so hard to bear. / I say that He was Christ, who wrought to bless . . ."' He broke off. 'I've been wanting to write that for three years.'

'Perhaps you should be glad you didn't.'

The light faded from Owen's face. 'Sorry?'

'Well, don't you think it's rather easily said? "I say that He was Christ"?'

'You m-mean you d-didn't m-mean it?'

'Oh, I meant it. The book isn't putting one point of view, it's charting the – the *evolution* of a point of view. That's probably the first poem that even attempts to look at the war realistically. And that one doesn't go nearly far enough.' He paused. 'The fact is Christ isn't on record as having lobbed many Mills bombs.'

'No, I s-see what you m-mean. I've been thinking about that quite a b-bit recently.'

Sassoon scarcely heard him. 'I got so sick of it in the end. All those Calvaries at crossroads just sitting there waiting to be turned into symbols. I knew a man once, Potter his name was. You know the miraculous crucifix stories? *"Shells falling all around, but the figure of Our Lord was spared"*? Well, Potter was so infuriated by them he decided to start a one-man campaign. Whenever he saw an undamaged crucifix, he used it for target practice. You could hear him for miles. "ONE, TWO, THREE, FOUR, Bastard on the Cross, FIRE!" There weren't many miraculous crucifixes in Potter's section of the front.' He hesitated. 'But perhaps I shouldn't be saying this? I mean for all I know, you're –'

'I don't know what I am. But I do know I wouldn't want a f-faith that couldn't face the facts.'

Sassoon became aware that Owen was standing at his elbow, almost like a junior officer. 'Why don't you sit down?' he said, waving him towards the bed. 'And tell me your name. I take it this one's for you?'

'Yes. Wilfred. Wilfred Owen.'

Sassoon blew on his signature and closed the book. 'You say you've been thinking about it?'

Owen looked diffident. 'Yes.'

'To any effect? I mean, did you reach any conclusions?'

'Only that if I were going to call myself a Christian, I'd have to call myself a pacifist as well. I don't think it's pos-sible to c-call yourself a C-Christian and . . . and j-just leave out the awkward bits.'

'You'll never make a bishop.'

'No, well, I think I can live with that.'

'And *do* you call yourself a pacifist?'

A long pause. 'No. Do you?'

'No.'

'It's funny, you know, I never thought about it at all in France.'

'No, well, you don't. Too busy, too tired.' Sassoon smiled. 'Too *healthy*.'

'It's not *just* that, though, is it? Sometimes when you're alone, in the trenches, I mean, at night you get the sense of something *ancient*. As if the trenches had always been there. You know one trench we held, it had skulls in the side. You looked back along and . . . Like mushrooms. And do you know, it was actually *easier* to believe they were men from Marlborough's army than to to to think they'd been alive two years ago. It's as if all other wars had somehow . . . distilled themselves into this war, and that makes it something you . . . almost can't challenge. It's like a very deep voice saying, *Run along, little man. Be thankful if you survive.*'

For a moment the nape of Sassoon's neck crawled as it had the first time Campbell talked about German spies; but this was not madness. 'I had a similar experience. Well, I don't know whether it is similar. I was going up with the rations one night and I saw the limbers against the skyline, and the flares going up. What you see every night. Only I seemed to be seeing it from the future. A hundred years from now they'll still be ploughing up skulls. And I seemed to be in that time and looking back. I think I saw our ghosts.'

Silence. They'd gone further than either of them had intended, and for a moment they didn't know how to get back. Gradually, they stirred, they looked round, at sunlight streaming over beds and chairs, at Sassoon's razor glinting on the washstand, its handle smeared with soap. Sassoon looked at his watch. 'I'm going to be late for golf.'

Immediately Owen stood up. 'Well, thanks for these,' he said, taking the books. He laughed. 'Thanks for writing it.'

Sassoon followed him to the door. 'Did you say you wrote?'

'I didn't, but I do.'

'Poetry?'

'Yes. Nothing in print yet. Oh, which reminds me. I'm editor of the *Hydra*. The hospital magazine? I was wondering if you could let us have something. It needn't be –'

'Yes, I'll look something out.' Sassoon opened the door. 'Give me a few days. You could bring your poems.'

This was said with such determined courtesy and such transparent lack of enthusiasm that Owen burst out laughing. 'No, I –'

'No, I mean it.'

'All right.' Owen was still laughing. 'They are quite short.'

'No, well, it doesn't lend itself to epics, does it?'

'Oh, they're not about the war.' He hesitated. 'I don't write about that.'

'Why ever not?'

'I s-suppose I've always thought of p-poetry as the opposite of all that. The ugliness.' Owen was struggling to articulate a point of view he was abandoning even as he spoke. 'S-Something to to t-take refuge in.'

Sassoon nodded. 'Fair enough.' He added mischievously, 'Though it does seem a bit like having a faith that daren't face the facts.' He saw Owen's expression change. 'Look, it doesn't matter what they're about. Bring them anyway.'

'Yes, I will. Thank you.'

Prior watched the amber lights winking in his beer. He was sitting in the shadowy corner of a pub in some sleazy district of Edinburgh. He didn't know where he was. He'd walked miles that evening, not admitting even to himself what he was looking for, and gradually the winding, insidious streets had led him deeper and deeper into a neighbourhood where washing hung, grey-white, from stacked balconies, and the smell of steak frying reminded him of home.

Remembering the smell, his stomach rumbled. He'd

had nothing to eat all evening, except a packet of peanuts. Crumbs of salt still clung to his lips, stinging the cracks where the skin had dried during his asthma attack. It was worth it, though, just to sit quietly, to listen to voices that didn't stammer, to have his eyes freed from the ache of khaki.

No theory. He'd lied to Rivers about that. It was a point of honour with him to lie to Rivers at least once during every meeting. He drained his glass and went out into the night.

A little way down the street was a café. He'd passed it on his way to the pub and been tempted to go in, but the door had opened and the breath of hot, damp, dirty, dish-water-smelling air had decided him against it. Now, though, he was too hungry to care. He went in, noticing how the inner windows dripped from condensation, how the damp air insinuated itself into the spaces between his uniform and his skin. A short silence fell. Nobody in an officer's uniform was likely to be inconspicuous or welcome here. He would eat something, fish and chips, quickly and then go.

A group of women was sitting at the next table. Three of them were young, one older, thirty-five, forty perhaps, with blackened stumps for teeth. As far as he could make out from the conversation her name was Lizzie, and the others were Madge, the blonde, pretty one, Betty, who was dark and thin, and Sarah, who had her back to him. Since they all had a slightly yellow tinge to their skin, he assumed they were munitions workers. Munition*ettes*, as the newspapers liked to call them. Lizzie was keeping the younger girls entertained with a string of stories.

'There's this lass and she's a bit simple and she lived next door to a pro – well you know what a pro is.' Lizzie glanced at him and lowered her voice. 'So she's standing at the door this day, and the pro's coming up the street, you know, *dressed to death*. So she says, "Eeh," she says, "you're always lovely dressed." She says, "You've got beautiful clothes." And she says, "I *love* your hats." So the pro says, "Well, why don't you get yourself down the town like I do?" She says, "If a man winks at you, wink back and go with him and let him have what he wants and charge him 7/6. And go to R & K Modes and get yourself a hat." So the next day the pro's coming up the street again. "Hello." "Hello." She says, "D' y' *get* a hat?" She says, "*Nah.*" "Well, did you not do as I telled you?" She says, "Why of course I did." She says, "I went down the town and there was a man winked at us and I winked back. He says, 'Howay over the Moor.'" So she says, "I gans over the Moor with him," she says, "and I let him have what he wanted. He says, 'How much is that?' I says, '7/6.' He says, 'Hadaway and shite,' and when I come back he'd gone.'"

The girls shrieked with laughter. He looked at them again. The one called Madge was very pretty, but there was no hope of winkling her out of the group, and he thought he might as well be moving on. As soon as his meal arrived, he began stuffing limp chips and thickly battered fish into his mouth, wiping the grease away on the back of his hand.

'You'll get hiccups.'

He looked up. It was Sarah, the one who'd been sitting with her back to him. 'You'll have to give us a surprise, then, won't you?'

'Drop me key down your back if you like.'

'That's nose bleeds, Sarah,' Betty said.

'She knows what it is,' said Lizzie.

Madge said, 'Hiccups, you're supposed to drink from the other side of the cup.'

She and Prior stared at each other across the table.

'But it's a con, isn't it?' he said. 'You can't do it.'

''Course you can.'

'Go on, then, let's see you.'

She dipped her small, straight nose into her cup, lapped, spluttered and came up laughing and wiping her chin. Betty, obviously jealous, gave her a dig in the ribs. 'Hey up you, you're gonna gerrus slung out.'

The café owner was eyeing them from behind the till, slowly polishing a glass on a distinctly grubby-looking tea towel. The girls went back to their tea, bursting into minor explosions of giggles, their shoulders shaking, while Prior turned back and finished his meal. He was aware of Sarah beside him. She had very heavy, very thick, dark-brown hair, but all over the surface, in a kind of halo, were other hairs, auburn, copper, chestnut. He'd never seen hair like that before. He looked at her, and she turned around and stared at him, a cool, amused stare from greenish eyes. He said, 'Would you like a drink?'

She looked at her cup.

'No, I meant a proper drink.'

'Pubs round here don't let women in.'

'Isn't there a hotel?'

'Well, there's the Cumberland, but . . .'

The other women looked at each other. Lizzie said, 'Howay, lasses, I think our Sarah's clicked.'

The three of them got up, said a good-natured 'good-night' and tripped out of the café, only bursting into giggles again after they'd reached the pavement.

'Shall we go, then?' said Prior.

Sarah looked at him. 'Aye, all right.'

Outside, she turned to him. 'I still don't know your name.'

'Prior,' he said automatically.

She burst out laughing. 'Don't you lot *have* Christian names?'

'Billy.' He wanted to say, and I'm not 'you lot'.

'Mine's Sarah. Sarah Lumb.' She held out her hand to him in a direct, almost boyish way. It intrigued him, since nothing else about her was boyish.

'Well, Sarah Lumb, lead on.'

Her preferred drink was port and lemon. Prior was startled at the rate she knocked them back. A flush spread across her cheeks in a different place from the rouge, so that she looked as if her face had slid out of focus. She worked in a factory, she said, making detonators. Twelve-hour shifts, six days a week, but she liked the work, she said, and it was well paid. 'Fifty bob a week.'

'I suppose that's something.'

'Too bloody right it is. I was earning ten bob before the war.'

He thought what the detonators she made could do to flesh and bone, and his mind bulged as a memory threatened to surface. 'You're not Scottish, though, are you?'

'No, Geordie. Well, what *you*'d call Geordie.'

'Did your dad come up looking for work?'

'No, they're still down there. I'm in lodgings down the road.'

Ah, he thought.

'"*Ah*," he thinks.' She looked at him, amused and direct. 'I think you're a bad lad.'

'No, I'm not. Nobody bad could be *that* transparent.'

'That's true.'

'Haven't you got a boyfriend?'

'What do you think?'

'I don't think you'd be sitting here if you had.'

'Oh, I might be one of these two-timing lasses, you never know.' She looked down into her glass. 'No, I haven't got one.'

'Why not? Can't all be blind in Scotland.'

'Perhaps I'm not on the market.'

He didn't know what to make of her, but then he was out of touch with women. They seemed to have changed so much during the war, to have expanded in all kinds of ways, whereas men over the same period had shrunk into a smaller and smaller space.

'I did have one,' she said. 'Loos.'

Odd, he thought, getting up and going to the bar to buy more drinks, that one word should be enough. But then why not? Language ran out on you, in the end, the names were left to say it all. Mons, Loos, Ypres, the Somme. Arras. He paid and carried the drinks back to their table. He thought that he didn't want to hear about the boyfriend, and that he was probably going to anyway. He was right there.

'I was in service at the time. It didn't . . .' Her voice became very brisk. 'It didn't seem to sink in. Then his mate came to see me. You weren't supposed to have followers. "Followers" – that's how old-fashioned she was. Especially *soldiers*. "Oh my *deah*." So anyway he come to the front door and . . .' She waved her hand languidly. 'I sent him away. Then I nipped down the basement and let him in the back.' She took a swig of the port. 'It was *our* gas,' she said, red-lidded. 'Did *you* know that?'

'Yes.'

'Our own bloody gas. After he'd gone, you know, I couldn't believe it. I just walked round and round the table and it was like . . . You know when you get a tune stuck in your head? I just kept on thinking, our gas. Anyway after a bit she come downstairs, and she says, "Where's tea?" I says, "Well, you can see for yourself. It's not ready." *We-ell*. First one thing was said and then another and in the end I did, I let her have it. She says, "You'd be making a great mistake to throw this job away, you know, Sarah." I says, "Oh, aye?" She says, "We don't say 'aye', Sarah, we say 'yes'." I says, "All right," I says, "'*yes*'. But 'aye' or 'yes', it's still ten bob a week and you put it where the monkey put the nuts." Same night I was packing me bags. No testimonial. And you know what that would've meant before the war?' She looked him up and down. 'No, I don't suppose you do. Anyway, I turned up at home and me Mam says, "I've no sympathy, our Sarah," she says. "You should have fixed him while you had the chance," she says. "And made sure of the pension. Our Cynthia had her wits about her," she says. "Why couldn't you?" And of course our Cynthia's sat there. Would you believe *in weeds*? I thought, aw to hell with this. Anyway, a couple of days after, I got on talking to Betty – that's the dark girl you saw me with just now – and we decided to give this a go.'

'I'm glad you did.'

She brooded for a while over her empty glass. 'You know, me Mam says there's no such thing as love between men and women. Love for your bairns, yes. Love for a man? *No*.' She turned to him, almost aggressively. 'What do *you* think?'

'I don't know.'

'Well, that makes two of us, then, 'cause I'm buggered if I do.'

'But you loved –'

'Johnny? I can't remember what he looked like.

Sometimes his face pops into me mind, like when I'm thinking about something else, but when I *want* to see it, I can't.' She smiled. 'That's the trouble with port and lemon, isn't it? Truth pours out.'

He took the hint and bought another.

By the time they left the pub she'd drunk enough to need his arm.

'Which way's your lodgings?'

She giggled. 'Won't do you any good,' she said. 'My landlady's a dragon. Fifty times worse than me Mam.'

'Shall we go for a walk, then? I don't fancy saying goodnight, just yet, do you?'

'All right.'

They turned away from the lighted pavements, into the darkness of a side street. He put his arm around her, inching his hand further up until his fingers rested against the curve of her breast. She was tall for a woman, and they fitted together, shoulder and hip. He hardly had to shorten his stride. As they walked, she glanced down frequently at her shoes and stockings, admiring herself. He guessed she more usually wore boots.

They came upon a church with a small churchyard around it. Gravestones leant together at angles in the shadow of the trees, like people gossiping. 'Shall we go in there for a bit?'

He opened the gate for her and they went in, into the darkness under the trees, treading on something soft and crunchy. Pine needles, perhaps. At the church door they turned and followed the path round, till they came to a tall, crumbling, ivy-covered wall. There, in the shadows, he pulled her towards him. He got her jacket and blouse unbuttoned and felt for her breast. The nipple hardened against his palm, and he laughed under his breath. She started to say something, but he covered her mouth with his own, he didn't want her to talk, he didn't want her to tell him things. He would have preferred not even to know her name. Just flesh against flesh in the darkness and then nothing.

'I know what *you* want,' she said, pulling away from him.

Instantly he let her go. '*I* know what I want. What's wrong with *that*? I've never forced anybody.' He turned away from her and sat on a tombstone. 'And I don't go on about it either.'

'Then you're a man in a million.'

'I know.'

'Big-headed bugger.'

'Don't I even get a cuddle?' He patted the tombstone. 'No harm in that.'

She came and sat beside him, and after a while he got his arms around her again. But he didn't feel the same way about it. Now, even as he lowered his head to her breast, he was wondering whether he wanted to play this particular game. Whether it was worth it. He tugged gently at her nipple, and felt her thighs loosen. Instantly, his doubts vanished. He pressed her back on to the tombstone and moved on top of her. Cradling her head on his left arm, he began the complicated business of raising her skirts, pulling down her drawers, unbuttoning his breeches, all while trying to maintain their position on a too-short and sloping tombstone. At the last moment she cried 'No-o-o' and shoved him hard off the tombstone into the long grass. He sat for a while, his back against the stone, picking bits of lichen off his tunic. After a while he yawned and said, 'Short-arsed little buggers, the Scots.'

She looked down at the tombstone, which did seem

rather small. 'Oh, I don't know. Everybody was shorter in them days.' You could just make out the word 'Beloved', but everything else was covered in lichen or crumbled away. She traced the word with her fingertip. 'I wonder what they think.'

'Down there? Glad to see a bit of life, I should think. Not that they've seen much.'

She didn't reply. He turned to look at her. Her hair had come down, way past her shoulders, he was glad she didn't wear it short, and there was still that amazing contrast of the dark brown velvety mass and its halo of copper wire. He was being stupid. She'd let him have it in the end, and the more he bellyached about it now, the longer he'd have to wait. He said, 'Come on, one kiss, and I'll walk you home.'

'Hm.'

'No, I mean it.'

He gave her a teasingly chaste kiss, making sure he was the first to pull away. Then he helped her dust down her skirt and walked her back to her lodgings. On the way she insisted they stop in the doorway of a shop, and she crammed her hair up into her hat, with the help of the few hairpins she'd managed to retrieve. 'There'd be eyebrows raised if I went in like this.'

'Can I see you again?'

'You know where I live. Or you will do.'

'I don't know your times off.'

'Sunday.'

'I'll come over on Sunday, then, shall I? If I come mid morning, we could have a bite to eat in Edinburgh and then go somewhere on the tram.'

She looked doubtful, but the thought of being collected from her lodgings by an officer was too much for her. 'All right.'

They walked on. She stopped outside the door and raised her face. Oh, no, he thought. No fumbling on doorsteps. He lowered his head until his forehead rested against hers. 'Goodnight, Sarah Lumb.'

'Goodnight, Billy Prior.'

After a few paces he turned and looked back. She was standing on the step, watching him walk away. He raised his hand, and she waved slightly. Then he turned and walked briskly on, looking at his watch and thinking, Christ. Even if he found a taxi *immediately* he still couldn't be back at Craiglockhart before the main doors were locked. Oh well, he thought, I'll just have to face it.

*   *   *

'Aren't *you* going to start?'

'I imagine Major Bryce has dealt with the matter?'

'You could say. He's confined me to the hospital for a fortnight.'

Rivers made no comment.

'Don't you think that's rather *severe*?'

'It wasn't a simple matter of being late back, was it? Matron says she saw you in town, and you were not wearing your hospital badge.'

'I wasn't wearing the badge because I was looking for a girl. Which – *as you may or may not know* – is not made easier by going around with a badge stuck on your chest saying I AM A LOONY.'

'I gather you also made some rather disrespectful remarks about Matron. Everything from the size of her bosom to the state of her hymen. If you make remarks like that to the CO, what do you *think* is going to happen?'

Prior didn't reply, though a muscle throbbed in his jaw.

Rivers looked at the pale, proud, wintry face and thought oh God, it's going to be another one of those.

Prior said, 'Aren't you going to ask me if I got one?'

'One what?'

'Girl. Woman.' When Rivers didn't immediately reply, Prior added, '*Wo-man?*'

'No, I wasn't going to ask.'

'You amaze me. I should've thought that was par for the course.'

Rivers waited.

'*Questions*. On and on and bloody on.'

'Would you like to leave it for today?'

'No.'

'You're sure?'

'Quite sure.'

'All right. We'd got to the time immediately following the April 23rd attack. Have you made any progress beyond that?'

'No.'

'Nothing at all?'

'No.' Prior's hands were gripping the arms of his chair. 'I don't want to talk about this.'

Rivers decided to humour him. 'What do you want to talk about?'

'Something you said earlier on. It's been bothering me ever since. You said officers don't suffer from mutism.'

'It's rare.'

'How many cases?'

'At Craiglockhart? You, and one other. At Maghull, where I was treating private soldiers, it was by far the commonest symptom.'

'Why?'

'I imagine . . . Mustism seems to spring from a conflict

between *wanting* to say something, and knowing that if you *do* say it the consequences will be disastrous. So you resolve it by making it physically impossible for yourself to speak. And for the private soldier the consequences of speaking his mind are always going to be far worse than they would be for an officer. What you tend to get in officers is stammering. And it's not just mutism. All the physical symptoms: paralysis, blindness, deafness. They're all common in private soldiers and rare in officers. It's almost as if for the . . . the labouring classes illness *has* to be physical. They can't take their condition seriously unless there's a physical symptom. And there are other differences as well. Officers' dreams tend to be more elaborate. The men's dreams are much more a matter of simple wish fulfilment. You know, they dream they've been sent back to France, but on the day they arrive peace is declared. That sort of thing.'

'I think I'd rather have their dreams than mine.'

'How do you know?' Rivers said. 'You don't remember your dreams.'

'You still haven't said why.'

'I suppose it's just a matter of officers having a more complex mental life.'

Prior reacted as if he'd been stung. 'Are you serious? You honestly believe that that *gaggle* of noodle-brained half-wits down there has a complex mental life? Oh, *Rivers*.'

'I'm not saying it's *universally* true, only that it's *generally* true. Simply as a result of officers receiving a different and, for the most part, more prolonged education.'

'*The public schools.*'

'Yes. The public schools.'

Prior raised his head. 'How do I fit into that?'

'We-ell, it's interesting that you were mute and that

you're one of the very few people in the hospital who *doesn't* stammer.'

'It's even more interesting that you do.'

Rivers was taken aback. 'That's d-different.'

'How is it different? Other than that you're on that side of the desk?' He saw Rivers hesitate. 'No, I'm not being awkward. I'm genuinely interested.'

'It's usually thought that neurasthenic stammers arise from the same kind of conflict as mutism, a conflict between wanting to speak and knowing that w-what you've got to say is not acceptable. Lifelong stammerers? Well. Nobody really knows. It may even be genetic.'

Prior smiled. 'Now that is lucky, isn't it? Lucky for you, I mean. Because if your stammer *was* the same as theirs – you might actually have to sit down and work out what it is you've spent fifty years trying not to say.'

'Is that the end of my appointment for the day, Mr Prior?'

Prior smiled.

'You know one day you're going to have to accept the fact that you're in this hospital because you're ill. Not me. Not the CO. Not the kitchen porter. *You.*'

After Prior had gone, Rivers sat for a while, half amused, half irritated. Now that his attention had been drawn to his stammer, it would plague him at intervals throughout the day. Bugger Prior, he thought. To be absolutely accurate, b-b-b-bugger Prior.

Prior had left slightly early, so Rivers had a few minutes before his next appointment. He decided to take a turn in the grounds. The grass was silvery with dew – his footsteps showed up dark along the path he'd come – but here and there the ground was beginning to steam. He sat on a bench under the trees, and watched two patients carrying scythes come round the corner of the building and run down the grassy slope that divided the gravel drive from the tennis courts. They looked, Rivers thought, almost comically symbolic: Time and Death invading the Arcadian scene. Nothing symbolic about the scythes, though. The blades over their shoulders glinted a wicked blue-grey. You could only wonder at an administration that confiscated cutthroat razors and then issued the patients with these. They set to work cutting the long grass by the hedges. There was a great deal of laughter and clumsiness at first, and not a few false starts, before their bodies bent into the rhythm of the task. Moths, disturbed from their daytime sleep, flickered all around them.

One took off his Sam Browne belt and then tunic, shirt and tie, casting them carelessly aside, and then went back to his scything, his dangling braces describing wide arcs around him as he swung the blade. His body was very pale, with a line round the neck, dividing white from reddish brown. The tunic had landed on the hedge, one sleeve raised as if beckoning. The other flung down his scythe and did the same. Work went more quickly now. Soon there was a gratifyingly large area of mown grass for them to look back on. They stood leaning on the scythes, admiring their work, and then one of them dived into the cut grass, winnowing his way through it, obviously excited by it in the way dogs sometimes are. He lay on his back, panting. The other man came across, said, 'Silly bugger,' and started kicking the grass all over him.

Rivers turned and saw Patterson – the Head of Office Administration – making his way at a steady pace down the slope to deliver the inevitable reprimand. King's regulations. No officer must appear in public with any garment missing. Patterson spoke to them, then turned away.

Slowly, they reached for their uniforms, pulled khaki shirts and tunics on to sweating bodies, buckled belts. It had to be done, though it seemed to Rivers that the scything went more slowly after that, and there was less laughter, which seemed a pity.

That night Rivers worked late, compiling lists of men to be boarded at the end of August. This was the most difficult task of any month, since it involved deciding which patients were fit to return to duty. In theory, the decision to return a man to service was taken by the Board, but since his recommendations were rarely, if ever, questioned, in practice his report determined the outcome. He was beginning to work on the first of these reports when there was a tap on the door. He called, 'Come in!'

Prior came into the room.

'Good evening,' Rivers said.

'Good evening. I came to say I'm sorry about this morning.'

The day had been so horrific in so many ways – culminating in a three-hour meeting of the hospital management committee – that Rivers had to grope for the memory. He said, 'That's all right.'

'It was stupid. Going on like that.'

'Oh, I don't know. We just caught each other at a bad moment.'

Prior lingered a few feet away from the desk. 'Why don't you sit down?' Rivers said.

'You must be tired.'

'Tired of paperwork.'

Prior's glance took in the list of names. 'The Boards.'

'The Boards.' He glanced at Prior. 'Not you this time.'

'Not enough progress.'

Rivers didn't immediately reply. He was watching Prior, noticing the pallor, the circles round the eyes. He had shadows under the shadows now. 'You have made progress. You've recovered almost all your memory *and* you no longer lose your voice.'

'You must wish I did.'

Rivers smiled. 'Don't exaggerate, Mr Prior. We both know if you *really* wanted to be offensive, you could do a hundred times better than you did this morning.' He waited for a reply. 'Couldn't you?'

Prior produced a curious rippling motion – half shrug, half flounce – and turned away. After a moment he looked sideways at Rivers. 'I did once think of asking you if you ever fucked any of your headhunters.'

'What stopped you?'

'I thought it was your business.'

Rivers pretended to consider the matter. 'That's true.'

'There's no point trying to be offensive, is there, if *that's* the only response you get?'

'You don't really want to be. You've always made a lot of *noise* about stepping over the line, but you've never actually done it.' Rivers smiled. 'Except just now, of course. And that was incredibly indirect.'

A short silence. Prior said, 'I wish I could go out. No, it's all right, I'm not asking. I'm just saying I wish I could. The nightmares get worse when I'm stuck indoors.' He waited. 'This is where you ask about the nightmares and I say I don't remember.'

'I know.'

Prior smiled. 'You never believed me, did you?'

'Should I have done?'

'No.'

'Do you want to talk about them now?'

'I can't. Look, they're just . . .' He laughed. '"*Standard issue battle nightmares. Potty officers for the use of.*" Nothing you won't have heard a hundred times before.'

'Except?'

'Except nothing.'

A long silence.

'Except that *sometimes* they get muddled up with sex. So I wake up, and . . .' He risked a glance at Rivers. When he spoke again, his voice was casual. 'It makes it really quite impossible to *like* oneself. I've actually woken up once or twice and wondered whether there was any point going on.'

And you might well do it, Rivers thought.

'That's why I was so furious when they got you up in the middle of the night.'

Easy to hand out the usual reassurances about the effects on young men of a celibate life, but not particularly helpful. Prior was becoming unmistakably depressed. It was doing him no good to wait for his CO's letter, which might anyway turn out to contain nothing of any great moment. 'We could try hypnosis now, if you liked.'

'Now?'

'Yes, why not? It's the time we're least likely to be interrupted.'

Prior's eyes flickered round the room. He licked his lips. 'It's odd, isn't it? When you said most people were frightened, I didn't believe you.'

'What frightens them,' Rivers said carefully, 'is the belief that they're putting themselves completely in the therapist's power. That he can make them do anything, even things they'd normally consider ridiculous or even immoral. But that isn't true, you remain your*self* throughout. Not that I shall be trying to make you do anything

23

ridiculous or immoral.' He smiled. 'In spite of being the terror of the South Seas.'

Prior laughed, but his face tightened again immediately.

'We can leave it, if you like,' Rivers said gently.

Deep breath. 'No. I can't pester you for it and then turn it down.'

'If it turns out to be . . .' Rivers groped for a sufficiently bland word, '*distressing*, I'll give you something to make you sleep. I mean, you won't have to face up to the full implications tonight.'

'All right. What do we do?'

'You relax. Sit back in the chair. That's right. Shoulders. Come on, like this. Now your hands. Let the wrists go. Comfortable? I want you to look at this pen. No, don't raise your head. Raise your eyes. That's right. Keep your eyes fixed on the pen. I'm going to count down from ten. By the time I get to zero, you'll be in a light sleep. All right?'

Prior nodded. He looked profoundly sceptical. Like most bloody-minded people he assumed he would be a poor subject for hypnosis. Rivers thought he'd be very easy. 'Ten . . . Nine . . . Eight . . . Seven . . . Your eyelids are heavy now. Don't fight it, let them close. Six . . . Five . . . Four . . . Three . . . Two . . .'

He woke to a dugout smell of wet sandbags and stale farts. He curled his toes inside his wet boots and felt the creak and sag of chicken wire as he turned towards the table. The usual jumble: paper, bottles, mugs, the black-boxed field telephone, a couple of revolvers – all lit by a single candle stuck to the wood in a pool of its own grease. A barely perceptible thinning of the darkness around the gas curtain told him it must be nearly dawn. And sure enough, a few minutes later Sanderson lifted the curtain and shouted, 'Stand-to!' The bulky forms on the other bunks stirred, groaned, groped for revolvers. Soon they were all trying to climb out of the dugout, difficult because rain and recent near-hits had turned the steps into a muddy slide. All along the trench men were crawling out of funk holes. He clumped along the duckboards to his position, smelling the green, ratty, decomposing smell, stretching the muscles of his face into a smile whenever the men looked up. Then an hour of standing, stiff and shivery, watching dawn grow.

He had first trench watch. He gulped a mug of chlorine-tasting tea, and then started walking along to the outermost position on their left. A smell of bacon frying. In the third fire bay he found Sawdon and Towers crouched over a small fire made out of shredded sandbags and candle ends, coaxing the flames. He stopped to chat for a few minutes, and Towers, blinking under the green mushroom helmet, looked up and offered him tea. A quiet day, he thought, walking on. Not like the last few days, when the bombardment had gone on for seventy hours, and they'd stood-to five times expecting a German counter-attack. Damage from that bombardment was everywhere: crumbling parapets, flooded saps, dugouts with gagged mouths.

He'd gone, perhaps, three fire bays along when he heard the whoop of a shell, and, spinning round, saw the scrawl of dusty brown smoke already drifting away. He thought it'd gone clear over, but then he heard a cry and, feeling sick in his stomach, he ran back. Logan was there already. It must have been Logan's cry he heard, for nothing in that devastation could have had a voice. A conical black hole, still smoking, had been driven into the side of the trench. Of the kettle, the frying-pan, the carefully tended fire, there was no sign, and not much of Sawdon and Towers either, or not much that was recognizable.

There was a pile of sandbags and shovels close by, stacked against the parapet by a returning work party. He reached for a shovel. Logan picked up a sandbag and held it open, and he began shovelling soil, flesh and splinters of blackened bone into the bag. As he shovelled, he retched. He felt something jar against his teeth and saw that Logan was offering him a rum bottle. He forced down bile and rum together. Logan kept his face averted as the shovelling went on. He was swearing under his breath, steadily, blasphemously, obscenely, inventively. Somebody came running. 'Don't stand there gawping, man,' Logan said. 'Go and get some lime.'

They'd almost finished when Prior shifted his position on the duckboards, glanced down, and found himself staring into an eye. Delicately, like somebody selecting a particularly choice morsel from a plate, he put his thumb and forefinger down through the duckboards. His fingers touched the smooth surface and slid before they managed to get a hold. He got it out, transferred it to the palm of his hand, and held it out towards Logan. He could see his hand was shaking, but the shaking didn't seem to be anything to do with him. 'What am I supposed to do with this gob-stopper?' He saw Logan blink and knew he was afraid. At last Logan reached out, grasped his shaking wrist, and tipped the eye into the bag. 'Williams and me'll do the rest, sir. You go on back now.'

He shook his head. They spread the lime together, sprinkling it thickly along the firestep, throwing shovelfuls at a bad patch of wall. When at last they stood back, beating the white dust from the skirts of their tunics, he wanted to say something casual, something that would prove he was all right, but a numbness had spread all over the lower half of his face.

Back in the dugout he watched people's lips move and was filled with admiration for them. There was a sense of joy in watching them, of elation almost. How complex those movements were, how amazing the glimpses of teeth and tongue, the movement of muscles in the jaw. He ran his tongue along the edges of his teeth, curved it back, stroked the ridged palate, flexed his lips, felt the pull of skin and the stretching of muscles in his throat. All present and correct, but how they combined together to make sounds he had no idea.

It was Logan who took him to the casualty clearing station. Normally it would have been his servant, but Logan asked if he could go. They thumped and splodged along cheerfully enough, or at least Prior was cheerful. He felt as if nothing could ever touch him again. When a shell whined across, he didn't flinch, though he knew the Germans had an accurate fix on both communication trenches. They marched from stinking mud to dryish duckboards, and the bare landscape he sensed beyond the tangles of rusty wire gradually changed to fields. Clumps of brilliant yellow cabbage weed, whose smell mimics gas so accurately that men tremble, hung over the final trench.

In the clearing station he sat down, Logan beside him. Lying on the floor was a young man wounded in the back who seemed hardly to know that they were there. From time to time he moaned, 'I'm cold, I'm cold,' but when the doctor came in, he shook his head and said there was nothing he could do. 'There's no need for you to stay,' he said to Logan. 'He'll be all right.' So they shook hands and parted. He sat down on the bench again and tried to think back over the events that had brought him there, but found he could remember very little about them. Two of his men were dead, he remembered that. Nothing else. Like the speechlessness, it seemed natural. He sat on the bench, his clasped hands dangling between his legs, and thought of nothing.

Rivers watched the play of emotions on Prior's face as he fitted the recovered memory into his past. He was unprepared for what happened next.

'*Is that all?*' Prior said.

He seemed to be beside himself with rage.

'I don't know about *all*,' Rivers said. 'I'd've thought that was a traumatic experience by any standards.'

Prior almost spat at him. 'It was *nothing*.'

He put his head in his hands, at first, it seemed, in bewilderment, but then after a few moments he began to cry. Rivers waited a while, then walked round the desk and offered his handkerchief. Instead of taking it, Prior seized Rivers by the arms, and began butting him in the chest, hard enough to hurt. This was not an attack, Rivers realized, though it felt like one. It was the closest Prior could come to asking for physical contact. Rivers was reminded of a nanny goat on his brother's farm, being lifted almost off her feet by the suckling kid. Rivers held Prior's shoulders, and after a while the butting stopped. Prior raised his blind and slobbery face. 'Sorry about that.'

'That's all right.' He waited for Prior to wipe his face, then asked, 'What did you think happened?'

'I didn't know.'

'Yes, you did. You *thought* you knew.'

'I knew two of my men had been killed. I thought . . .' He stopped. 'I thought it must've been my fault. We were in the same trenches we'd been in when I first arrived. The line's terrible there. It winds in and out of brick stacks. A lot of the trenches face the wrong way. Even in daylight with a compass and a map you can get lost. At night . . . I'd been there about a week, I suppose, when a man took out a patrol to see if a particular dugout was occupied at night. Compasses don't work, there's too much metal about. He'd been crawling round in circles for God knows how long, when he came upon what he thought was a German wiring party. He ordered his men to open fire. Well, all hell was let loose. Then after a while somebody realized there were British voices shouting on both sides. Five men killed. Eleven injured. I looked at his face as he sat in the dugout and he was . . . You could have done *that* and he wouldn't've blinked. Before I'd always thought the worst thing would be if you were wounded and left out there, but when I saw his face I thought, no. This is the worst thing. And then when I couldn't remember anything except that two of my men had been killed, I thought it had to be something like that.' He looked up. 'I couldn't see what else I'd need to forget.'

'Then you must be relieved.'

'Relieved?'

'You did your duty. You've nothing to reproach your-self with. You even finished cleaning the trench.'

'I've cleaned up dozens of trenches. I don't see why that would make me break down.'

'You're thinking of breakdown as a reaction to a single traumatic event, but it's not like that. It's more a matter of . . . *erosion*. Weeks and months of stress in a situation where you can't get away from it.' He smiled. 'I'm sorry to sound so impersonal. I know how you hate being "the patient".'

'I don't mind in the least. I just want to understand why it happened. You see what I find so difficult is . . . I don't think of myself as the kind of person who breaks down. And yet time and time again I'm brought up hard against the fact that I *did*.'

'I don't know that there is "a kind of person who breaks down". I imagine most of us could if the pressure were bad enough. I know I could.'

Prior gazed round the room in mock amazement. 'Did the wallpaper speak?'

Rivers smiled. 'I'll tell them to give you a sleeping tablet.'

At the door Prior turned. 'He had very blue eyes, you know. Towers. We used to call him the Hun.'

After making sure Prior got his sleeping tablet, Rivers went upstairs to his own room and began to undress. He tugged at his tie, and as he did so caught sight of himself in the looking-glass. He pulled down his right lid to reveal a dingy and blood-shot white. *What am I supposed to do with this gob-stopper?* He released the lid. *No need to think about that.* If he went on feeling like this, he'd have to see Bryce and arrange to take some leave. It'd reached the point where he woke up in the morning feeling almost as exhausted as he had done when he went to bed. He sat on the edge of the bath and began to take his boots off. *Ye will surely say unto me this proverb. Physician, heal thyself.* One of his father's favourite texts. Sitting, bored and fidgety, in the family pew, Rivers had never thought it an odd choice, though now he wondered why it cropped up as frequently as it did. Fathers remain opaque to their sons, he thought, largely because the sons find it so hard to believe that there's anything in the father worth seeing. Until he's dead, and it's too late.

Mercifully, doctors are also opaque to their patients. Unless the patient happens to be Prior.

Rivers finished undressing and got into the bath. He lay back, eyes closed, feeling the hot water start to unravel the knots in his neck and shoulders. Not that Prior was the only patient to have found him . . . Well. Rather less than opaque. He remembered John Layard, and as always the memory was painful, because his treatment of Layard had ended in failure. He told himself there was no real resemblance between Layard and Prior. What made Prior more difficult was the constant *probing*. Layard had never probed. But then Layard hadn't thought he needed to probe. Layard had thought he knew.

Lying with his eyes closed like this, Rivers could imagine himself back in St John's, hearing Layard's footsteps coming across the court. What was it he'd said? 'I don't see you as a *father*, you know.' Looking up from the rug in front of the fire. Laughing. 'More a sort of . . . *male mother*.' He *was* like Prior. The same immensely shrewd eyes. X-ray eyes. The same outrageous frankness.

Why should he remember that? It was because of that ridiculous image of the nanny goat that had flashed into his mind while Prior was butting him in the stomach. He disliked the term 'male mother'. He thought he could remember disliking it even at the time. He distrusted the implication that nurturing, even when done by a man, remains female, as if the ability were in some way borrowed, or even stolen, from women – a sort of moral equivalent of the *couvade*. If that were true, then there was really very little hope.

He could see why Layard might use the term. Layard's relationship with his father had been difficult, and he was a young man, without any personal experience of fathering.

Though fathering, like mothering, takes many forms beyond the biological. Rivers had often been touched by the way in which young men, some of them not yet twenty, spoke about feeling like fathers to their men. Though when you looked at what they *did*. Worrying about socks, boots, blisters, food, hot drinks. And that perpetually harried expression of theirs. Rivers had only ever seen that look in one other place: in the public wards of hospitals, on the faces of women who were bringing up large families on very low incomes, women who, in their early thirties, could easily be taken for fifty or more. It was the look of people who are totally responsible for lives they have no power to save.

One of the paradoxes of the war – one of the many – was that this most brutal of conflicts should set up a relationship between officers and men that was . . . domestic. Caring. As Layard would undoubtedly have said, maternal. And that wasn't the only trick the war had played. Mobilization. The Great Adventure. They'd been *mobilized* into holes in the ground so constricted they could hardly move. And the Great Adventure – the real life equivalent of all the adventure stories they'd devoured as boys – consisted of crouching in a dugout, waiting to be killed. The war that had promised so much in the way of 'manly' activity had actually delivered 'feminine' passivity, and on a scale that their mothers and sisters had scarcely known. No wonder they broke down.

In bed, he switched off the light and opened the curtains. Rain, silvery in the moonlight, streaked the glass, blurring the vista of tennis courts and trees, gathering, at the lower edge of the pane, into a long puddle that bulged and overflowed. Somebody, on the floor below, screamed. Rivers pulled the curtains to, and settled down to sleep, wishing, not for the first time, that he was young enough for France.

* * *

Sarah watched the grey trickle of tea creep up the sides of her cup. The tea-lady looked at it, doubtfully. 'That strong enough for you, love?'

'It'll do. Long as it's warm and wet.'

'My God,' Betty Hargreave said. 'Virgin's pee. I can't drink that.'

Madge nudged Sarah sharply in the ribs. 'No, well, it wouldn't be very appropriate, would it?'

'Hey up, you'll make us spill it.'

They went to the far end of the top trestle table and squeezed on to the bench. 'Come on, move your bums along,' Madge said. 'Let two little 'uns in.'

Lizzie collected her Woodbines and matches, and shuffled along. 'What happened to your young man, then, Sarah?'

'Didn't bloody show up, did he? I was sat an hour on Sunday all dolled up and nowhere to go.'

'*Aw,*' Lizzie said.

'Probably just as well,' said Madge. 'At least now you know what he was after.'

'I knew what he was after. I just want to know why he's not still after it.'

'Didn't get it, then?' Betty said, bringing her cup to the table.

'No, he bloody did not.'

'He was good-looking, though, wasn't he?' said Madge.

'All right, I suppose.'

Betty laughed. 'Better fish in the sea, eh, Sarah?'

'Aye, and they can stop there 'n' all. Not interested.'

A whoop of incredulity. Sarah buried her nose in her cup and then, as soon as she felt their attention had been withdrawn, looked at the window. You couldn't really see what it was like outside because the glass was frosted, but here and there raindrops clung to the panes, each with its crescent moon of silver. She wished she was outside and could feel the rain on her face. It would have been nice to have gone to the seaside yesterday, she thought. Bugger him, why didn't he show up?

The others were talking about Lizzie's husband, who'd thrown her into a state of shock by announcing, in his last letter, that he was hoping to come home on leave soon.

'I haven't had a wink of sleep since,' said Lizzie.

'You're getting yourself into a state about nothing,' Betty said. 'First of all he mightn't get it, and second, they sometimes only give them a few days. Ten to one, he'll get no further than London.'

'Aye, and he'll be pissed as a newt.'

'Well, better pissed down there than up here.'

'Don't you want to see him?' asked Sarah.

'I do not. I've seen enough of him to last me a lifetime. Aye, I know what you're thinking. You think I'm hard, don't you? Well I *am* hard and so would you be.' Lizzie's yellow face showed two bright spots of colour on the cheekbones. 'Do you know what happened on August 4th 1914?'

Sarah opened her mouth.

'I'll tell you what happened. *Peace* broke out. The only little bit of peace *I*'ve ever had. No, I don't want him back. I don't want him back on leave. I don't want him back when it's over. As far as I'm concerned the Kaiser can keep him.' She lowered her chin, brooding. 'I'll tell you what I'm going to do. I'm going to get meself some false teeth, and I'm going to have a bloody good time.'

'Yes, well, you want to,' said Betty.

'She's been on about them teeth as long as I've known her,' said Madge. 'You want to stop talking about it, and go and do it. You can afford it. All this won't last, you know.' She jerked her thumb at the room full of overall-clad women. 'It's too good to last.'

'It's not the money that bothers me.'

'He'd give you gas,' said Madge. 'You're never going to look anything while you've got them in your mouth. And you're never going to feel right either for the simple reason you're swallowing all the corruption.'

'Yeh, I know. I will go.'

'Time, ladies,' the supervisor said. 'Time.'

'Eeh, it never is,' said Lizzie. 'Do you know, I'm bloody sure they fix that clock!'

'Three hours down,' said Sarah. 'Nine to go.'

All over the room yellow-skinned women were dragging themselves to their feet. As they were going up the stairs, Sarah fell into line beside Betty. Lizzie had nipped into the toilet to finish her cigarette.

'You think she's hard, don't you?' said Betty.

'Well, yes, I do a bit. When you think what he's going through.'

'Yes, well. You know when I was a kid we used to live next door to them, and it was thump thump thump half the bloody night, you'd've thought she was coming through the wall. Oh, and you used to see her in the yard next morning, and her face'd be all swelled up. "I fell over the coal scuttle," she used to say. Well, that used to get me Mam. "*He* knocks you about," she says, "and *you* go round apologizing for it," she says. "Where's the justice in that?" And mind you, she was right, you know.'

* * *

Sassoon was trying to decipher a letter from H. G. Wells when Owen knocked on his door.

'As far as I can make out, he says he's coming to see Rivers.'

Owen looked suitably impressed. 'He must be really worried about you.'

'Oh, it's not *me* he wants to talk about, it's his new book.' Sassoon smiled. 'You don't know many writers, do you?'

'Not many.'

And I, Sassoon thought, am showing off. Which at least was better than moaning about Gordon's death to somebody who had more than enough problems of his own. 'I don't suppose he'll come. They all talk about it, but in the end it's just too far. I sometimes wonder whether that's why they put me here. Whether it was a case of being sent to Rivers or just sent as far away as possible.'

'Probably Rivers. He gets all the awkward ones.' Owen stopped in some confusion. 'Not that you're –'

'Oh, I think I count as awkward. By any standard.' He handed a sheet of paper across. 'For the *Hydra*.'

'May I read it?'

'That's the general idea.'

Owen read, folded the paper and nodded.

To forestall possible effusions, Sassoon said quickly, 'I'm not satisfied with the last three lines, but they'll have to do.'

'I tried yesterday, but you were out.'

'I'd be with Rivers.' He smiled. 'Do you ever feel like strangling Brock?'

'No, I get on rather well with him.'

'I *get on* with Rivers. It's just . . . He picked up something I said at lunchtime about not being able to imagine the future. He doesn't often press, but my God when he does . . .'

'Why did he want you to talk about that?'

'Part of the great campaign to get me back to France. He wants me to put the protest in a longer perspective. You know, "What did you do in the Great War, Siegfried?" Well, I spent three very comfortable years in a loony-bin eating steamed pudding and playing golf. While *other people* – some of them rather close friends – got blown to smithereens. He wants me to admit I won't be able to bear it. What's more, he's probably right.'

'Think of the poems you could write.'

'Not war poems.'

Owen's expression darkened. 'There are other subjects.'

'Yes, of course.'

A slightly awkward pause. 'The trouble is he just knows more than I do. You know, he's very good . . . He tries to behave as if we're equal. But in the end he's a Gold Medallist of the Royal Society, and I left Cambridge without taking a degree. And now and again it shows.'

'That doesn't mean he's right.'

'No, but it does make it very difficult for me to keep my end up in a discussion.'

'Did you talk about after the war?'

'No. I can't, I've no plans. Do *you* know what you're going to do?'

'I'm going to keep pigs.'

'*Pigs?*'

'Yes. People think pigs are dirty, you know, but they're not. They're very clean animals, given half the chance. And it would combine so well with poetry, you see. Actually much better than teaching, because if you're teaching *properly* you're using the same part of your mind. But pig-keeping . . .'

'Perhaps we should go into partnership. It'd shut Rivers up.'

Owen, belatedly aware of being laughed at, blushed and didn't reply.

'No, well, I don't suppose I'd be much use with the pigs, but I may be able to help with the poems.' He nodded at Owen's tunic.

Owen extracted a sheaf of papers. 'I told you they were all short but actually there is one long one. Antaeus and and Hercules.' He handed the papers over. 'Do you know the legend? Antaeus is too strong for Hercules as long as he keeps his feet on mother Earth. But as soon as Hercules lifts him –'

'He's helpless. Yes, it rings a bell.' Sassoon started to read. After a few seconds he looked up. 'Why don't you get yourself a book? There's nothing worse than being watched by the Onlie Begetter.'

'Sorry.' Owen got up and pretended to look at the books on Sassoon's shelf.

At last Sassoon looked up. 'It's very good. Why Antaeus?'

'Oh, it's something Brock's keen on. He thinks we – the patients – are *like* Antaeus in the sense that we've been ungrounded by the war. And the way back to health is to re-establish the link between oneself and the earth, but understanding "earth" to mean society as well as nature. That's why we do surveys and things like that.'

'I thought all the dashing around was to keep your mind off it?'

'No, that's part of the treatment. Ergotherapy.'

'Well, it's an interesting idea. Though I don't know that being stuck in a dugout ever made *me* feel I was losing contact with the earth.'

Owen smiled. 'No, nor me. It does *work*, though.'

Sassoon picked up the next sheet. Craning his neck, Owen could just see the title of the poem. 'That's in your style,' he said.

'Yes. I . . . er . . . *noticed*.'

'No good?'

'Starts and ends well. What happened in the middle?'

'That's quite old, that bit. I wrote that two years ago.'

'They do say if you leave something in a drawer long enough it'll either rot or ripen.'

'The bit at the end . . . About "dirt". Those are the actual words.'

'Yes, and they could do with changing. I've just cut: "You sod" out of a poem. Those were *my* actual words.'

'So it's no good?'

Sassoon hesitated. 'It's not much good *at the moment*. I suppose the thing is, are you interested enough to go on?'

'Ye-es. I have to start somewhere. And I think you're right. It's mad not to write about the war when it's –'

'Such an *experience*.'

They looked at each other and burst out laughing.

'My only doubt is . . . The the *fact* that you admire somebody very much doesn't automatically mean they're a good model. I mean, I admire Wilde, but if I started trying to be witty and elegant and incisive, I'd probably fall flat on my face.'

'Yes, I see that. Well, not *that*. I mean I see the point. But I do think I can take something from you.'

'Fair enough.' Sassoon went back to his reading. 'I think you're probably right,' he said, after a while. 'If I do nothing else, I might help you get rid of some of this *mush*.'

'Some of the sonnets are quite early.'

'Puberty?' A long pause. Early sonnets fell like snow. 'Oh, now this is good. "Song of Songs."'

'That's last week.'

'*Is it?* Now you see what I mean about me not being necessarily the right model? *I* couldn't do this. And yet of it's kind it's absolutely perfect.'

Owen sat down. He looked as if his knees had buckled.

'I think that should go in the *Hydra*.'

'No.'

'Why not?'

'a. It's not good enough. b. Editors shouldn't publish their own work.'

'a. I'm a better judge of that than you are. *At the moment*. b. Rubbish. And c.' Sassoon leant across and snatched his own poem back. 'If you don't publish *that*, you can't have this.'

Owen seemed to be contemplating a counter-attack.

'd. I'm bigger than you are.'

'All right, I'll print it.' He took Sassoon's poem back. 'Anonymously.'

'Cheat.' Sassoon was shuffling Owen's papers together. 'Look, why don't you have a go at . . .' He peered at the title. '"The Dead-Beat"? Work at it till you think you've made some progress, then bring it back and we'll have a go at it together. It's not too traumatic, is it? That memory.'

'Good heavens, no.'

'How long do you spend on it? Not that one, I mean generally?'

'Fifteen minutes.' He saw Sassoon's expression change. 'That's *every day*.'

'Good God, man, that's no use. You've got to sweat your guts out. Look, it's like drill. You don't wait till you *feel* like doing it.'

'Well, it's certainly a new approach to the Muse. "Number from the left! Form fours! Right turn!"'

'It works. I'll see you – shall we say Thursday? After dinner.' He opened the door and stood aside to let Owen past. 'And I shall expect to find *both* poems in the *Hydra*.'

* * *

After Prior had been waiting for perhaps five minutes, the lodging house door opened and Sarah stood there. 'You've got a nerve,' she said, beginning to close the door.

Prior put a finger in the crack. 'I'm here now.'

'Which is more than you were last week. Go on, *shift*.'

'I couldn't come last week. I was so late back they kept me in.'

'Bit strict, aren't they? Your *parents*.'

Too late, he remembered the lies he'd told. He pointed to the blue badge on his tunic. 'Not parents. The CO.'

The door stopped shutting.

'I know it sounds stupid, but it *is* the truth.'

'Oh, all right, I believe you.' Her eyes fell on the badge. 'And if you're getting yourself upset about that, don't bother. I knew anyway.'

'How did you know?' What had he been doing? *Drooling?*

'You don't think you're the only one takes it off, do you?

They all do. Betty says she had a young man once, she never saw him wearing it. Mind you, knowing Betty, I shouldn't think she saw him wearing much at all.'

By day, the yellowness of her skin astonished him. It said a lot for her that she was still attractive, that she managed to wear it like a rather dashing accessory.

'There is just one thing,' she said, coming out into the porch. 'If I do go out with you, I want one thing clear at the start. I think you must've got a very wrong impression of me the other night. Knocking all that port back.' She raised her eyes to his face. 'I don't usually drink much at all.'

'I know that. You were gone too quick for somebody that was used to it.'

'Right, then. Long as you know. I'll get me jacket.'

He waited, looking up and down the hot street. A trickle of sweat had started in his armpits. From deep inside the house came a woman's voice raised in anger.

'Me landlady,' Sarah said, coming back. 'Belgian, married a Scot, the poor sod. I don't think he knew what he was getting. Still, she only charges a shilling for the laundry, and when you think the sheets come off the bed bright yellow you can't complain about that.'

He felt at home with her, with this precise delineation of the cost of everything, which was not materialistic or grasping, but simply a recognition of the boundaries and limitations of life. 'I thought we'd get out of Edinburgh,' he said. 'It's too hot.'

Most of Edinburgh was using this last weekend in August to escape the city, not deterred by a sallow tinge to the sky that suggested the hot, sticky weather might break into thunder before the day was out. The train was packed, but he managed to get her a seat, and stood near by. She smiled

up at him, but in this rackety, sweating box it was impossible to talk. He looked at the other passengers. A trio of girls
out on a spree, a young mother with a struggling toddler
tugging at her blouse, a middle-aged couple whose bodies
sagged together. Something about that stale intimacy sharp-
ened his sense of the strangeness, the separateness of Sarah's
body. He was so physically aware of her that when the knee
of his breeches brushed against her skirt he felt as if the
contact had been skin on skin.

A ganglion of rails, the train juddering over points, and
then they were slowing, and people were beginning to stir
and clutch bags, and jam the aisles. 'Let's wait,' he said.

Sarah pressed against him, briefly, to let the woman and
her child past, and then he sat beside her as the train
emptied. After a while she reached down and touched his
hand.

They took their time walking to the sea. At first he was
disappointed, it was so crowded. Men with trousers rolled
up to show knobbly legs, handkerchiefs knotted over sweating scalps, women with skirts tucked up to reveal volu-
minous bloomers, small children screaming as the damp
sand was towelled off their legs. Everywhere people
swirling their tongues round ice-cream cones, biting into
candy-floss, licking rock, sucking fingers, determined to
squeeze the last ounce of pleasure from the day. In his
khaki, Prior moved among them like a ghost. Only Sarah
connected him to the jostling crowd, and he put his hand
around her, clasping her tightly, though at that moment
he felt no stirring of desire. He said, 'You wouldn't think
there was a war on, would you?'

They walked down to the water's edge. He felt quite
callous towards her now, even as he drew her towards him
and matched his stride to hers. She belonged with the

43

pleasure-seeking crowds. He both envied and despised her, and was quite coldly determined to *get* her. They owed him something, all of them, and she should pay. He glanced at her. 'Shall we walk along?'

Their linked shadows, dumpy and deformed, stretched across the sand. After a while they came to an outcrop of rock, and, clambering over it, found they'd left the crowded part of the beach behind. Sarah took off her jacket and then, with a great fuss and pleas not to look, her shoes and stockings as well. She paddled at the water's edge, where the waves seethed between her toes.

'I don't suppose you're allowed to take anything off?' she said, looking back at him, teasing.

'Not a thing.'

'Not even your boots?'

'No, but I can wade. I always paddle with me boots on.'

He didn't expect her to understand, or if she did, to admit it, but she turned on him at once. 'Boots have a way of springing a leak.'

'Not mine.'

'Oh, you'd be different, I suppose?'

Until now the air had been so still it scarcely moved against the skin. But now small gusts began to whip up the sand, stinging patches of bare skin. Prior looked back the way they'd come. The sun was past its height. Even the little mounds of worm-casts had each its individual shadow, but what chiefly struck him was the yellowing of the light. It was now positively sulphurous, thick with heat. They seemed to be trapped, fixed, in some element thicker than air. Black figures, like insects, swarmed across the beach, making for the shelter of the town.

Sarah, too, had turned to look back. He said quickly, 'No, don't let's go back. It'll blow over.'

'You think *that's* gunna blow over?'

Reluctantly he said, 'Do you *want* to go back?'

'We'd be drenched before we got there. Anyway, I like storms.'

They stood looking out to sea, while the yellow light deepened. There was no difference now between his skin colour and hers. Suddenly Sarah clutched her head. 'What's happening?'

He could hardly believe what he saw. The coppery wires on the surface of her hair were standing straight up, in a way he had never believed any human hair could do. He pulled his cap off, and winced at the tingling in his scalp.

'What is it?' Sarah said.

'Electricity.'

She burst out laughing.

'No, I mean it.'

Lightning flickered once, illuminating her yellow skin. 'Come on,' Prior said.

He snatched her hand and started to run with her towards the shelter of some bushes. Scrambling up the last slope, he staggered, and would have fallen if he hadn't grabbed a clump of marram grass. He felt a sharp pain, and, bringing his hand up, saw a smear of blood on the palm. Sarah pushed him from behind. They stumbled down the other side of the slope, just as a sudden fierce thickening of rain blinded them, and the first rumblings of thunder came.

A dense thicket of buckthorn offered the only possible shelter. Prior stamped down the nettles and thistles that thronged the gaps, and then held the thorns back for Sarah to crawl inside. He followed her in. They crouched down, the rain scarcely reaching them through the thick roof of thorn, though the wind rocked and beat the bush. Prior looked round. The ground was dry, and very bare, the thorn too thick to allow anything else to grow.

Sarah was feeling her hair. 'Is it all right?'

'It's going down.'

'So's yours.'

He grinned. ''S not surprising. Storm took me mind right off it.'

She laughed, but refused to reply. Prior was remembering childhood games, making dens. An interior like this, so dark, so private, so easily defended, would have been a real find. Mixed with this distinctly childish excitement another excitement was growing. He no longer felt hostile to her, as he'd done back there in the crowd. They seemed to have walked away from all that. It was ages since he'd made love. He felt as he sometimes did coming out of the line, listening to the others talk and sometimes joining in, what they were going to do and how many times they were going to do it, though as far as he knew everybody else's experience was like his own. The first time was almost always a disappointment. Either stuck at half mast or firing before you reached the target. He didn't want to think about Sarah like this.

Sarah rolled over on to her elbow and looked at him. 'This is nice.'

He lay beside her. A few splashes of rain found his upturned face. After a while he touched her hand and felt her fingertips curl round his. Through the thickness in his throat, he said, 'I'm not pushing, but if you wanted to, I'd make sure it was all right.'

After a while he felt her fingers creep across his chest, insinuating themselves between the buttons of his tunic. He kissed her, moving from her lips to her breasts, not looking at her, not opening his eyes, learning her with his tongue, flicking the nipples hard, probing the whorled darkness of her navel, and then on down, down, across the smooth marble of her belly into the coarse and springy turf. His nostrils filled with the scent of rock pools at low tide. He slipped his hands underneath her, and lifted her, until her whole pelvis became a cup from which he drank.

Afterwards they lay in silence, enjoying the peace, until footsteps walking along the coastal path warned them that the storm was over. The buckthorn scattered raindrops over them, as they crawled out on to the grass.

They beat sand and twigs from each other's clothes, then started to walk back along the coastal path.

'What we need is something to warm us up,' Prior said. 'We can't go anywhere looking like this.'

They stopped on the outskirts of the town, and tried more seriously to set themselves to rights. They went to a pub, and leant back against the wooden seat, nudging each other under the table, drunk with their love-making and the storm and the sense of having secrets.

'I can feel your voice through the wood,' Sarah said.

Abruptly, the joy died. Prior became quite suddenly depressed. He pushed his half-finished meal away.

'What is it?'

'Oh, I was remembering a man in my platoon.' He looked at her. 'Do you know, he sent the same letter to his wife every week for two years.'

Sarah felt a chill come over her. She didn't know why she was being told this. 'Why?'

'Why not?'

'How do you know he did?'

'Because I had to censor it. I censored it every week. We read all their letters.'

He could see her not liking this, but she kept her voice light. 'Who reads yours?'

'Nobody.' He looked at her again. 'They rely on our sense of honour. Oh, we're supposed to leave them open so the CO *can* read them if he wants to, but it would be thought *frightfully bad form* if he did.' Prior had slipped into his mock public school voice, very familiar to Rivers.

Sarah took it at face value. 'You lot make me sick,' she said, pushing her own plate away. 'I suppose nobody else's *got* a sense of honour?'

He preferred her like this. On the beach, she was only too clearly beginning to think that something had happened that mattered. He wasn't going to admit that. A few grains of sand in the pubic hair, a mingling of smells. Nothing that a prolonged soak in the tub wouldn't wash away. 'Come on,' he said, putting down a tip. 'We'd better be getting back.'

*   *   *

'This is getting to be a habit, isn't it?'

Prior, hands twined round the iron bars of the bedhead, smiled without opening his eyes. 'Not one I enjoy.'

He hadn't regained the weight he'd lost during his last stay in sick bay. The ribs showed clearly through the stretched skin. 'You were lucky to get back. When did it start?'

'On the train. It was jam-packed. Everybody smoking.'

'Lucky the young woman with you kept her head.'

'Poor Sarah. I don't think she's ever had anybody pass out on her before.'

'You realize you won't have the sick bay to yourself this time?' Rivers indicated the other bed. 'Mr Willard.'

'The legless wonder. Yes, we've met.'

'Don't you have any sympathy for anybody else?'

'Are you suggesting I have any for myself?' He watched Rivers fold the stethoscope. 'You know what you were saying about the greater mental complexity of officers? How long do you think it'll take you to convince that particular specimen of *complexity* that it hasn't actually got a broken spine?'

'How's your voice, Mr Prior?'

Prior took a moment to register the direct hit. 'Fine. Problem over, I think. I miss it. I used to enjoy my little Trappist times.'

'Oh, I can believe that. I've often thought how nice it would be to retreat into total silence now and again.'

'What do you mean "how nice it would be"? You do it all the time.'

'I've arranged for a consultant to come and see you. A Dr Eaglesham. He'll be in some time this week.'

'Why?'

'I need a measurement of your vital capacity.'

'Demonstrations twice nightly.'

'The *other* vital capacity. Try to get some rest now. Sister Duffy tells me you had a bad night.'

Rivers had got to the door before Prior called him back. '*Why* do you need it?'

'This is the second time this has happened in six weeks. I don't think we can let you go in front of a Medical Board without drawing their attention to your *physical* condition.'

'If you're thinking of wangling permanent home service, I don't want it.'

'I'm not thinking of "wangling" anything.' Rivers looked down at Prior and his expression softened. 'Look, if this is what happens when you're exposed to cigarette smoke on a train, how would you cope with gas?'

'Well, *obviously*, I'm affected at lower concentrations than anybody else. But then so what? I can be the battalion canary.' A pause. 'I'm not the only one with asthma.'

'No, I'm sure you're not. I'm *told* there are cases of active TB in the trenches. It doesn't mean it's a good idea.'

'I want to go back.'

A long silence.

'You can't talk to anybody here,' Prior said. 'Everybody's either lost somebody, or knows somebody who has. They don't want the truth. It's like letters of condolence. "Dear Mrs Bloggs, Your son had the side of his head blown off by a shell and took five hours to die. We did manage to give him a decent Christian burial. Unfortunately that particular stretch of ground came under heavy bombardment the day after, so George has been back to see us five or six times since then." They don't want that. They want to be told that George – or Johnny – or whatever his name was, died a quick death and was given a decent send off.' He said deliberately, 'Yesterday, at the seaside, I felt as if I came from another planet.'

'You can talk to people here.'

'It's the last thing this lot want to talk about. The point is, I'm better.'

'That's for the Board to decide.'

'You mean, *you*.'

'No-o. The Board. How are the nights? I mean apart from the asthma? I know last night was bad.'

'I just refuse to play this game. I haven't enough *breath* to answer questions you already know the answers to.'

'What's your *subjective* estimate of your nights?'

'Better.'

'Good. That was Sister Duffy's impression too.'

'Oh *well*, then . . .' Prior glowered. 'There's another reason I want to go back. Rather a nasty, selfish little reason, but since you clearly think I'm a nasty selfish little person that won't come as a surprise. When all this is over, people who didn't go to France, or didn't do well in France – people of my generation, I mean – aren't going to count for anything. This is the Club to end all Clubs.'

'And you want to belong.'

'Yes.'

'You already do.'

'I broke down.'

'And that's why you want to go back? You're ambitious, aren't you?'

Prior didn't answer.

'No reason why you shouldn't be. What do you want to do?'

'Politics.' He started back-tracking immediately. 'Of course, it's probably useless. You can't get anywhere in this shitting country without an Oxford or Cambridge degree.'

'Rubbish.'

'Easily said.'

'Not easily said at all. I didn't go to either.'

Prior looked surprised.

'I got typhoid in my last year at school. We couldn't afford Cambridge without the scholarship. No, you can certainly get on without. And things'll be freer after the war. If only because hundreds of thousands of young men have been thrown into contact with the working classes in a way they've never been before. That has to have some impact.'

'Careful, Rivers. You're beginning to sound like a Bolshevik.'

'I'm just trying to give you some faith in your own

abilities. And by the way, I do *not* think you are a nasty selfish little person.'

Prior scowled ferociously, probably to hide his pleasure.

'I'll try to be here when Dr Eaglesham comes. Meanwhile, do you think you could try to get on with Willard?'

Rivers was going on leave. He hadn't been down to dinner for the past few days, but he was there tonight, Sassoon saw, looking rather better than he'd done recently, though still very tired. The MO's table was the noisiest in the room. Even at this distance you could distinguish Brock's high, reedy voice, MacIntyre's broad Glaswegian, Bryce's Edinburgh, Ruggles's American, and Rivers, who, when he got excited in a discussion, as he often did, sounded rather like a soda-water syphon going off. Nobody, listening to him now, would have thought him capable of those endless silences.

Fothersgill, his long nose twitching fastidiously, had started to complain about the soup. 'Nay, verily,' he said. 'A man knoweth not what manner of thing he eateth.' He laughed as he said it, the laugh of a man who takes small discomforts very seriously indeed. Sassoon, marooned between two particularly bad stammerers, felt no need to take part in the conversation. Instead, he twisted round in his seat and looked for Owen, remembering the last poem he'd been shown. '*Out there, we've walked quite friendly up to Death;/Sat down and eaten with him, cool and bland –/Pardoned his spilling mess-tins in our hand . . .*' Precisely, Sassoon thought. And now we complain about the soup. Or rather, *they* do.

After dinner he went straight to Owen's room. 'Do you mind?' he said.

Owen was already clearing papers from the chair. 'No, come in.'

'Have you got anything for me?'

'This.'

Sassoon took the sheet and read the whole poem through twice, then returned to the first two lines.

> What minute-bells for these who die so fast?
> – Only the monstrous/solemn anger of our guns.

'I thought "passing" bells,' Owen said.

'Hm. Though if you lose "minute" you realize how weak "fast" is. "Only the monstrous anger . . ."'

'"Solemn"?'

'"Only the solemn anger of our guns." Owen, for God's sake, this is War Office propaganda.'

'No, it's not.'

'Read that line.'

Owen read. 'Well, it certainly isn't meant to be.'

'I suppose what you've got to decide is who are "these"? The British dead? Because if they're *British*, then *our* guns is . . .'

Owen shook his head. 'All the dead.'

'Let's start there.' Sassoon crossed out 'our' and pencilled in 'the'. 'You're sure that's what you want? It isn't a minor change.'

'No, I know. If it's "the", it's got to be "monstrous".'

'Agreed.' Sassoon crossed out 'solemn'. 'So:

> What passing-bells for these who die . . . so *fast*?
> – Only the monstrous anger of the guns.

'Well, there's nothing wrong with the second line.'

'"In herds"?'

'Better.'

They worked on the poem for half an hour. The wind had been rising all evening, and the thin curtain billowed in the draught. At one point Sassoon looked up and said, 'What's that noise?'

'The wind.' Owen was trying to find the precise word for the sound of shells, and the wind was a distraction he'd been trying to ignore.

'No, *that*.'

Owen listened. 'I can't hear anything.'

'That tapping.'

Owen listened again. 'No.'

'Must be imagining things.' Sassoon listened again, then said, 'They don't *wail*. They hiss.'

'No, these are going right over.'

'That's right. They hiss.' He looked at Owen. 'I hear hissing.'

'*You* hear tapping.'

The wind went on rising all evening. By the time Sassoon left Owen's room, it was wailing round the building, moaning down chimneys, snapping branches off trees with a crack like rifle fire. All over the decayed hydro, badly fitting windows rattled and thumped, and Sassoon, passing several of his 'fellow breakdowns' in the corridor, thought they looked even more 'mental' than usual.

His own room was empty. He got into bed and lay reading while he waited for Fothersgill to return from his bridge session. As soon as he entered the room, Sassoon rolled over and pretended to be asleep. A tuneless whistling ensued, punctuated by grunts as Fothersgill bent over his shaving mirror and tweezed hairs out of his nostrils.

At last the light was out. Sassoon lay on his back, listening to the roar of wind and rain. Again he heard tapping, a distinct, purposeful sound, quite unlike the random buffeting of the wind. On such a night it was impossible not to think of the battalion. He listened to the surge and rumble of the storm, and his mind filled with memories of his last few weeks in France. He saw his platoon again, and ran through their names – not a particularly difficult feat, since no fewer than eight of them had been called Jones. He recalled his horror at their physique. Many of them were almost incapable of lifting their equipment, let alone of carrying it mile after mile along shelled roads. He'd ended one march pushing two of them in front of him, while a third stumbled along behind, clinging to his belt. None of the three had been more than five feet tall. You put them alongside an officer – almost any officer – and they seemed to be almost a different order of being. And as for their training. One man had arrived in France not knowing how to load a rifle. He saw them now, his little band, sitting on bales of straw in a sun-chinked barn, while he knelt to inspect their raw and blistered feet, and wondered how many of them were still alive.

The windows banged and rattled, and again, in a brief lull, he thought he heard tapping. There were no trees close enough to touch the glass. He supposed there might be rats, but then whoever heard of rats tapping? He tossed and turned, thinking how stupid it was not to be able to sleep here, in safety and comfort, when in France he'd been able to sleep anywhere. If he could sleep on a firestep in drenching rain, surely he could sleep now . . .

He woke to find Orme standing immediately inside the door. He wasn't surprised, he assumed Orme had come to rouse him for his watch. What did surprise him, a little, was that he seemed to be *in bed*. Orme was wearing that very pale coat of his. Once, in 'C' company mess, the CO had said, 'Correct me if I'm wrong, Orme, but I have always assumed that the colour of the British Army uniform is khaki. Not . . . *beige*.' 'Beige' was said in such Lady Bracknellish tones that Sassoon had wanted to laugh. He wanted to laugh now, but his chest muscles didn't seem to work. After a while he remembered that Orme was dead.

This clearly didn't worry Orme, who continued to stand quietly by the door, but Sassoon began to think it ought to worry him. Perhaps if he turned his head it would be all right. He stared at the window's pale square of light, and when he looked back Orme had gone.

Fothersgill was awake. 'Did you see anybody come in?' Sassoon asked.

'No, nobody's been in.' He turned over and within a few minutes was snoring again.

Sassoon waited for the rhythm to be firmly established, then got out of bed and walked across to the window. The storm had blown itself out, though twigs, leaves and even one or two larger branches, scattered across the tennis courts, bore witness to its power. The palms of his hands were sweating and his mouth was dry.

He needed to talk to Rivers, though he'd have to be careful what he said, since Rivers was a thorough-going rationalist who wouldn't take kindly to tales of the supernatural, and might even decide the symptoms of a war neurosis were manifesting themselves at last. Perhaps they were. Perhaps this was the kind of hallucination he'd had in the 4th London, but no, he didn't believe that. His nocturnal visitors *there* had come trailing gore, pointing to amputations and head wounds, rather like the statues of medieval saints pointing to the instruments of their martyrdom. This had been so restrained. Dignified. And it hadn't followed on from a nightmare either. He thought back, wanting to be sure, because he knew this was the first question Rivers would ask. No, no nightmare. Only that tapping at the window before he went to sleep.

He got dressed and sat on the bed. At last eight o'clock came, and the hospital became noisy as the shifts changed. Sassoon ran downstairs. He felt certain Rivers would go to his office to check the post before he left, and there might just be time for a few words. But when he tapped on the door, a passing orderly said, 'Captain Rivers's gone, sir. He left on the six o'clock train.'

So that was that. Sassoon went slowly upstairs, unable to account for his sense of loss. After all, he'd known Rivers was going. And he was only going for three weeks. Fothersgill was still asleep. Sassoon collected his washbag and went along to the bathroom. He felt almost dazed. As usual he turned to lock the door, and as usual remembered there were no locks. At times like this the lack of privacy was almost intolerable. He filled the basin, and splashed his face and neck. Birds, sounding a little stunned as if they too needed to recover from the night, were beginning, cautiously, to sing. He looked at his face in the glass. In this half-light, against white tiles, it looked scarcely less ghostly than Orme's. A memory tweaked the edges of his mind. Another glass, on the top landing at home, a dark, oval mirror framing the face of a small, pale child. Himself. Five years old, perhaps. Now why did he remember that? Birds had been singing, then, too. Sparrows, twittering in the ivy. A day of shouts and banged doors and tears in rooms he was not allowed to enter. The day his father left home. Or the day he died? No, the day he left. Sassoon smiled, amused at the link he'd discovered, and then stopped smiling. He'd joked once or twice to Rivers about his being his father confessor, but only now, faced with this second abandonment, did he realize how completely Rivers had come to take his father's place. Well, that didn't matter, did it? After all, if it came to substitute fathers, he might do a lot worse. No, it was all right. Slowly, he lathered his face and began to shave.

POCKET PENGUINS